Little, Brown and Company

Hachette Book Group
1290 Avenue of the Americas, New York, NY 10104
Visit us at lb-kids.com

LB kids is an imprint of Little, Brown and Company.
The LB kids name and logo are trademarks of Hachette Book Group, Inc.

The publisher is not responsible for websites (or their content) that are not owned by the publisher.

First Edition: November 2015

Library of Congress Control Number: 2015939598

ISBN 978-0-316-30000-1

10 9 8 7 6 5 4 3 2 1

APS

Printed in China

minionsmovie.com

minions
Snow Day

By Brandon T. Snider
Illustrated by Ed Miller

Based on the Motion Picture Screenplay
Written by Brian Lynch

LITTLE, BROWN & COMPANY
LB kids

These little guys are Minions.
Kevin is the thinker. He's protective of his pals.
Stuart dreams of becoming a rock star.
And Bob has a curious spirit!

It's way too cold to go outside. The Minions will become ice cubes in an instant! Better to stay in their cave and wait for the chilly winter to pass.

Being inside for too long has Kevin, Stuart, and Bob going a little crazy. Hopefully a new master will come along soon and save them from their boredom. In the meantime, they've got one another, and that's pretty cool. Friends are the best.

Kevin feels a drop of water on his head. That means the sun is out! Its heat is warming up the cave and causing the ice to melt. Soon the Minions will be able to go outside without freezing their goggles off.

They'll be able to do so many fun things once they're outside. Just imagine!

Time to break out their snow gear. Stuart and Bob could use a little help choosing the right clothes to wear. Don't worry. Kevin knows what to do. Bundle up warm and tight, Minions. It's cold out there.

Now that the Minions are properly
suited up, it's time for the final touch.
A stick? Nope.
A rake? Not quite. Sorry, Bob.
A shovel? *DING, DING, DING!*
We have a winner.

Watch out, winter! Here come the Minions!

Now it's time to push that big boulder aside so they can leave the cave and enjoy the warm day. This isn't going to be easy.

Ta-da!

Oh no! The Minions successfully move the boulder, but the cave entrance is blocked by snow. They'll have to dig their way through. It's a good thing they're prepared.

Ooh-la-la.

Oh?

There's one thing left to do.
The Minions begin digging their
tunnel to freedom. Look at Bob go!

The Minions' shoveling has created a series of crazy tunnels.

Check it out! Bob finds something hidden in the snowbank.

Bob discovers a bunch of his Minion buddies, and they're frozen solid! Don't panic. Bob knows the right thing to do. Kind of. Kevin and Stuart have their own ideas of how to help, just in case.

Once their friends have defrosted, Kevin, Stuart, and Bob welcome their old pals with open arms.

Yikes! Bob finds a polar bear trapped in the ice. Be careful, Minion. This discovery could mean trouble.

Ha-ha! Poochie!

Now that the Minions have dug themselves out of their icy home, they're ready to play. What should they do with all this extra snow? Hmmm.

Building an igloo is a difficult job. Thankfully, the Minions know how to work together.

Keep going, Stuart! Don't give up!

Be careful, Bob. Ice can be slippery.

Norbert, don't eat the ice!

Dave, Paul, Henry, Brian, and the other Minions follow Kevin's lead. He knows what to do.

The igloo is finally done! With pride, the Minions gather around their beautiful new creation. Not bad, huh?
Hey! Check out Bob!

Oooh!

There are so many cool things to discover inside the igloo.

While the Minions were working, the ice holding the polar bear melted. *Whoops!* Now he's looking for his next meal. Isn't he?

LOOKA!

The good news: The igloo is amazing.

The bad news: The polar bear agrees. Now the bear has made the Minions' wonderful ice fortress his home. He still looks hungry, so the Minions retreat to their ice cave.

Bob and Stuart think about how to remove the polar bear from their igloo. They gather the other Minions and show them their crazy ideas.

Snowman!

WHOOSH!

Luckily, Kevin always has a plan!

Hmmm.

Kevin rallies his friends
to take back the igloo.
MINIONS ATTACK!

They've got their enemy on the run. VICTORY!
Or so they think. The Minions don't see the giant
shadow behind them. Whatever it is scared the bear
away with just one look.

Now that there isn't any danger, the Minions can
finally play in peace.

Bob makes a gigantic snow cone. Yummy.

Norbert creates his very own snow-Minion. Impressive.

Stuart is making snow angels. *Awww*, so cute.

What a great day!

While the others play, Kevin sees the real hero that saved them from the bear. But is it a friend or a foe? Or maybe, just maybe…it's…

Big...boss?

…a brand-new master! Kevin sure hopes it is. After all, the Minions deserve only the best.